Become a star reader

This three-level reading series is designed ☐ beginning readers and is based on popular Caillou episodes. The books feature common sight words used with limited grammar. Each book also offers a set number of target words. These words are noted in bold print and are presented in a picture dictionary in order to reinforce meaning and expand reading vocabulary.

Level 1

Little Star

For pre-readers to read along
- 125-175 words
- Simple sentences
- Simple vocabulary and common sight words
- Picture dictionary teaching 6 target words

Level 2
Rising Star

For beginning readers to read with support
- 175-250 words
- Longer sentences
- Limited vocabulary and more sight words
- Picture dictionary teaching 8 target words

Level 3
Super Star

For improving readers to read on their own or with support
- 250-350 words
- Longer sentences and more complex grammar
- Varied vocabulary and less-common sight words
- Picture dictionary teaching 10 target words

Text: adaptation by Rebecca Klevberg Moeller
All rights reserved.
Original story written by Marilyn Pleau-Murissi, based on the animated series CAILLOU
Illustrations: Eric Sévigny, based on the animated series CAILLOU

The PBS KIDS logo is a registered mark of PBS and is used with permission.

Chouette Publishing would like to thank the Government of Canada and SODEC
for their financial support.

Books
Tax Credit

Gestion
SODEC

Bibliothèque et Archives nationales du Québec and Library and Archives
Canada cataloguing in publication

Moeller, Rebecca Klevberg
Caillou, on stage: read with Caillou, level 3
Previously published as: My first play. 2009.
For children aged 3 and up.
ISBN 978-2-89718-447-6

1. Caillou (Fictitious character) - Juvenile literature. 2. Drama - Juvenile
literature. I. Sévigny, Éric. II. Pleau-Murissi, Marilyn. My first play. III. Title.

PN2037.M63 2017   j792   C2016-942527-4

Printed in China
10 9 8 7 6 5 4 3 2 1   CHO2004 MAY2017

Super Star

Level

3

On Stage

Text: Rebecca Klevberg Moeller, Language Teaching Expert
Illustrations: Eric Sévigny, based on the animated series

chouette dhx media

Caillou is at daycare. He is playing with his **friends**.

Their names are Clementine and Leo.

Anne is their **teacher**.
"Do you remember
what we are doing
today?" she says.

"Today we are putting on
a **play**!" Caillou answers.

"That's right!" their **teacher** says.
"Let's get ready!"
The **friends** are very **happy**.

First, the **friends** find clothes
to wear.

Caillou puts on a red hat.
Leo puts on a red nose.
Clementine puts on a blue hat.

"Remember, our **play** tells a story," says their **teacher**. "We must wear special clothes."

The **friends** get dressed
for the **play**.

Caillou is
the **sun**.

Clementine is
a **flower**.

Leo is a
rain **cloud**.

Next, the **friends** practice the **play**.
"I am a **flower**," Clementine says.
"I am the **sun**," Caillou says.
"I will make you **hot** and **thirsty**."

The **friends** must practice hard.
Later, they will be on a **stage**.

Their families will come to the **play**. They must do well!

The **stage** is ready.
The **friends** are ready.

The families are waiting.
Everyone is excited.
It is time for the **play**!

Clementine comes on the **stage**.
"I am a **flower**. I am waiting for the **sun**."
She looks for Caillou. But where is he?

Clementine repeats. "I am a **flower**. I am waiting for the **sun**." This time Caillou comes on the **stage**.

"I am the **sun**. I will warm you, **flower**," Caillou says.
"The **sun** is **hot**," the **flower** says.
"Now I am **hot** and **thirsty**!"

Next Leo comes on the **stage**.
"I am a rain **cloud**," he says.
"I will give you water."
"Thank you, Mr. **Cloud**,"
Clementine says.

The **play** is over.
Everyone liked it!

The **sun**, the **cloud**, and the **flower** are very **happy**!

Picture Dictionary

friends

teacher

play

happy

sun

flower

cloud

hot

thirsty

stage